CRY
IN THE
DARK

written and illustrated by

DEE SHULMAN

First published 2005 by
A & C Black Publishers Ltd
37 Soho Square, London, W1D 3QZ

www.acblack.com

ISBN 0-7136-7250-1

A CIP catalogue for this book is available from the British Library.

A&C Black uses paper produced with elemental chlorine-free
pulp, harvested from managed sustained forests.

Printed and bound in Great Britain by Bookmarque Ltd, Croydon

Chapter One

This has to be the worst day of my life.

Worse than the day I scored an own goal in the school semifinals. Worse than the day I had to wear a kilt at my aunty Gemma's wedding. Even worse than the day ... my dad left.

Today Martin is moving in. Martin. Smarmbin. Smart bin. Fart tin. He's my mum's boyfriend. I hate him. Of course Jack the prat (my stupid kid brother) thinks he's really, really nice. 'Cause Fartbin plays Frustration and Subbuteo with him. And buys him Happy Meals at McDonalds, and stuff. Jack doesn't even try to remember what it was like when Dad was still here.

And now Smarmbin thinks he can just march in and be our dad.

I kick the door. In the place I always kick it. There's a satisfying splintering noise as a bit more wood chips off.

'Ben – what are you doing?' Uh-oh – Mum's coming upstairs. Bum! She's coming in.

She looks at the door and sighs. 'I know you're not happy about Martin coming' – give her a prize for brilliant deduction – 'but when you get to know him I know you'll like him.'

'Never!' I spit.

The doorbell rings.

'That'll be him now!' Mum says with a sloppy smile on her face. 'You will try and be nice, Ben?'

'I'm always nice,' I say.

She skips off to answer the door.

I look out of the window. Solid blue sky. Could have been a fantastic day if Martin's car wasn't down there with its stupid boot open. A Vauxhall Cavalier. Sad! Dad drives a really cool silver-grey BMW: air con, electric windows, CD player, sunroof – the lot. Only I haven't seen it yet. He hasn't had it that long.

Well, only a few months, anyway. We were supposed to see it yesterday. Dad said he'd take us out for a ride. Promised. Jack and me dribbled a football up and down the path, waiting and watching for a silver streak to swish into our road. Until it was really late. Jack got cold and went in. But I was sure Dad would come. So I stayed by the gate. Willing the next car to be his.

It wasn't. Nor the next. Mum called out, 'Supper!' Dad was meant to have us back in time for supper. And we hadn't even gone yet. So I knew waiting was pointless. Dad wasn't coming.

I smashed the ball into a rose bush and slammed the front door shut. It nearly came off its hinges. I wish it had. Then Martin would have had to fix it! Martin's always fixing things.

His tacky little tool kit's been hanging round the house for months. And now the rest of his stuff'll be joining it.

I look back out of my window at Martin's car and I just want to throw something down on it. Smash it up. For a moment I consider my computer. A computer out of the window would wreck a car. Only I don't want to smash up my computer. Dad got it for me. Well, it's his old one.

I pick up a tin of marbles instead. That could cause some damage. I open my window. Then I duck. Martin's out there. He lifts a couple of boxes and heads back towards our house. I raise the tin and carefully aim.

Bum! Now Jack's down there too. What? I don't believe it – Mum's joined them! They're all bringing Martin's stuff in – like one big happy family. Martin is just locking the boot and he turns and looks up. He sees me looking down at him – and smiles!

Oh no! He's coming upstairs. He's going to come into my room! There's only one way out. Through the window.

I climb on to the sill. I'm the best climber in the class, maybe the whole year. I've been right to the top of the oak tree in Millfield park. Martin's right outside my room. I can hear him. Without thinking, I reach across from my windowsill on to the sill of the house next door.

Chapter Two

The windows are all boarded up. No one has lived here for ages. I stand on the sill for a minute, wondering what on earth I'm doing. But then I look down and see Martin's car below. My fury returns, and I grab at a rotten piece of wooden boarding. It comes away easily in my hand. Within seconds I've made a gap big enough to crawl through and I'm inside.

I can't see anything at all! I have to stand there waiting till my eyes get used to the dark. But my nose works fine. Which is not good. 'Cause there's this horrible smell. Sort of rotten. It's really cold too – all damp and clammy. I stare into the darkness and the shape of the room starts to appear. Hey – it's exactly the same as mine! Well, the same size anyway. Nothing much in it except a disgusting old mattress in the corner, with bits of straw sticking out. And a pile of rags on top. That's about it, apart from some old newspaper on the floor.

Oh *yuk*! There are *beetles* crawling up the walls! No wonder nobody ever comes to live here. What a dump! I fling myself back towards the window – I'm out of here.

Then my mate Amit's voice echoes round my head, *Scaredy Cat, Puke on the mat...* So I turn, hold my breath, and leap towards the landing, keeping well away from the crawling wall. I'm the White Rider in the HOUSE OF DOOM! I've made it through the Dreaded Beetle Room. What next? The landing floorboards could do with Martin and his trusty little tool kit! Every step makes them creak and wobble, and there are great holes where the boards have just rotted away. This is real White Rider territory...

What's that noise? I stand really still. My heart is thudding. Then I hear it again. It's a kind of sniffing. A cat, maybe? Or – a *rat*? I swallow. Beetles are one thing. Rats... Even the White Rider hates rats. I am just on the point of bolting back to the window, when the sound changes from sniffing to soft crying... Definitely human.

Maybe it's coming through the wall from our house. Maybe Martin has made Jack cry! I feel a wave of protective anger. But in my heart I know it doesn't sound like Jack, and it's definitely coming from downstairs. Very slowly I make my way down. The wood on the stairs splinters with every step. Just cross over this great big gap and CRUNCH! I'm falling through... I grab the banister, but it comes away in my hand. I clutch the stair above – it snaps in two. I'm still falling...

YEOW! Actually – amazingly, miraculously – I'm hardly hurt at all. I've landed on something soft – a pile of old rags. I rub my elbow, peering into the gloom, but suddenly I freeze. I can hear breathing! All sorts of House of Doom monsters flash through my mind but I force myself to look towards the sound. And then I see him: a boy, huddled in a corner, staring back at me.

'Did you fall through the stairs too?' I ask. He just gazes at me with a really shocked look on his face. 'Are you hurt?'

I peer through the dark at him. He's very thin, pretty small – not much bigger than Jack. And filthy. Well, it's hard to tell what's dirt and what's bruise. His skin is covered in bruises and cuts. He has this big dark lump on the side of his head, just by his eye. It's all sort of crusty with dry blood and pus. His hair is matted and stiff.

'Did you fall?' I ask again.

He's still looking at me. He's looking at me like I'm totally off my trolley. Then his eyes go sort of glazed, and he says, 'Been locked in...'

'Locked in?' I look around and see that we're in the cupboard under the stairs. There is a door but it has no handle. I push against it anyway. It's locked. I look around me, horrified. I'm in a kind of cell. And I don't want to know what's inside that metal bucket in the corner. 'Who locked you in?'

My words are drowned out by the sound of the front door slamming shut and heavy footsteps coming towards us. Then a man's slurred voice shouts, 'Who wants another beating? Look at this mess in here. I want it cleaned up NOW!'

He kicks against the door of the cupboard. The boy starts shaking, his eyes wide with fear. I hear a shooshing, clicking noise. 'He's taking off his belt,' the boy whispers. 'He's coming in.'

Looking at the boy, I know that this man isn't bringing us a can of coke and a bag of crisps. 'Quick!' I say. 'We can climb out through the hole in the ceiling,' and I start clambering up. The boy just huddles further back in the corner. The lock on the outside of the door rattles menacingly. 'Come on!' I squeak in terror.

The boy just shakes his head. 'No way out,' he says in the bleakest voice I've ever heard.

Suddenly the door is flung open and I'm not waiting. I grab on to the wood around the hole and, praying it won't give way, pull my body up through the gap. My feet dangle helplessly for a few seconds while I try to find something higher to grab on to. I hear the man immediately below me. My heart is beating so loud I think it'll give me away. I expect to feel my legs gripped and pulled down but, with one desperate tug, I manage to clear the cupboard and heave myself forward and up the stairs.

I don't think about rotten floorboards or keeping quiet, or the boy I've left behind. I just run. I climb out through the gap in the window boarding, across the sills and back through my own window. Which I slam shut. I stand in the middle of my bedroom floor, sweating, shaking, trying to get my breathing under control. Which might have been possible if I hadn't heard a noise even louder than my heartbeat. A knocking on my bedroom door…

He's come to get me.

I try to swallow. I can't. I watch as the door handle slowly turns. The door opens…

'Ben?' Martin stands in the doorway. I never thought I'd live to feel relief at the sight of Martin. I try to rearrange my expression. I fail.

'Ben? What's wrong? You look … terrified. Hey, you're not frightened of *me*, are you?' He looks really alarmed.

I can't help it. I just start to laugh. Nobody could be frightened of Martin. Not even a squirrel could be frightened of Martin. He tries to ignore my sniggering.

'I just popped up to say hello.' His voice tails off, but I carry on laughing. He looks so nerdy standing there, that I have to look down at the floor. I notice how colourful the rug I'm standing on is. And for some reason it makes me think of the dark, filthy floor of the room next door. NEXT DOOR! That boy!

I've got to do something. I look up. Martin has slipped out of the room. I run downstairs to find Mum.

Chapter Three

'What do you mean, you climbed across the windowsills to the house next door? You can't have done – I was only in your room a moment ago.'

'Well, it *was* only a moment ago. Honestly, Mum!'

'You're truthfully telling me that you crossed from your bedroom to the house next door just now? But your bedroom is six metres off the ground! What if you had fallen? Why would you do such a stupid thing?'

'Never mind why I did it. The thing is, I found this boy, locked in the cupboard under the stairs.'

'You found *what*?' Mum sits down.

'And he wouldn't follow me out of the hole when we heard the man coming back, and I think he's being beaten up right now. He was covered in bruises and filthy and—'

'Slow down, Ben, slow down. Now, tell me… From the beginning.'

And so I tell her, and she dials 999 and the next thing I know two police cars have screamed into our road, and uniformed men are hammering on the peeling front door of the house I've just escaped from. As half the street gather round to watch, the lock finally gives way and the door shudders open.

The policemen force their way through this massive pile of junk mail and shine torches all around. It's just as derelict as the upstairs. I show them the cupboard under the stairs. The door is bolted. One of them forces the rusty old bolt back, but the door doesn't open immediately. It's really stuck. 'This door hasn't been opened for years!' he says.

'But the man only just came in!' I tell him.

They've got the door open. They shine the torch around. The cupboard is totally empty. Except for a pile of rags.

'That's where I landed!' I yell. 'He's got to be here somewhere!' I search wildly round the cupboard. 'Hey, there's the hole I fell through!' I point up to the ceiling.

The policemen aren't impressed. 'Look, son,' one of them says irritably. 'Nobody's opened this cupboard door in ages. It was completely sealed up with dust and distemper. And there hasn't been anyone through this front door for years. Look at all this post. Look at the floor...'

Suddenly I see what he means. There is a thick layer of dust on all the surfaces. The only footprints are ours.

A couple of the policemen wander around upstairs, but none of them seem to believe me.

'He really was here...' I say weakly, as we all leave by the front door.

Three of them drive off in one car. The last policeman takes me back home. He has a few words with Mum and then calls me in.

'Now then,' he says, in this really stern voice, 'I don't know what's going on in that head of yours. Your mum says you're not a bad lad, so on this occasion we'll say no more about it. But I'm sure you know it's an offence to waste police time, and if you make up anything like this again, we will view it very differently.'

I'm standing there with Mum, Martin and Jack looking at me like I'm a book written in Cantonese. They're just staring. I suppose from their angle it all does look a bit weird. But it doesn't look exactly normal from my angle.

'I ... er ... need time to sort my head out,' I say, and bolt upstairs to my room.

•

I sit on my bed and try to work out what just happened.

About half an hour ago, I went next door and found a boy locked in the cupboard under the stairs. Fifteen minutes later there is no sign of him. What's going on? I write down the options:

① The boy's escaped.

② The man's taken him somewhere.

③ I dreamt it.

④ I saw a ghost.

⑤ I made the whole lot up.

As I sit there looking at the choices, only one of them seems totally impossible. I know I didn't make it all up. But the longer I consider, the more crazy it seems. The way Mum, Jack and Martin were staring at me... Maybe I *am* going loony.

I decide the healthiest thing to do is forget the whole episode ever happened. And hope that no one at school gets to hear about it.

Chapter Four

I stay in my room till Mum calls me to come and eat. I manage to get through the whole meal without looking at the others once. Martin does most of the talking. He talks about us all maybe going to France for our summer holiday. He talks to Jack about his teacher, his swimming, the book he's reading. He talks to Mum about the weekends he's working – Martin Smarmbin Do-Good Social Worker. He talks about the spaghetti we're eating and the different kinds of pasta he had when he went to Italy. He doesn't talk about the police, or the disappearing boy next door. No one does.

When we finish eating, I go straight up to my room again. I put a CD in the machine, lie down on my bed and … doze off.

When I wake up it's two am! I'm still lying on my bed fully clothed. I can tell Mum's been in, because there's a blanket covering me, and my light's been switched off. I sit up, wondering whether I should bother putting on my pyjamas, when I hear somebody coughing.

It must be Jack. No, it isn't Jack, it's not coming from Jack's room. It's coming from …

next door. 'You're dreaming,' I tell myself. 'This whole next-door thing is just a dream. Go back to sleep and it'll go away.' I get under the duvet and lie down again. Mmm... Lovely and warm...

There it is again. A sick, hacking cough. I sit up. My heart is thumping. My brain is saying, 'Lie down, go to sleep.' But my brain isn't in charge now.

I am rummaging through my desk drawer for the torch. Got it. The battery's a bit flat but it's good enough. Before I can change my mind, I'm on the windowsill, edging my way across to the one next door. This time it's easier, because I know where the gap in the boarding is.

I'm in. I stand by the window trying to get my torch to switch on.

'Are you an angel?' whispers a voice from the corner of the room.

I nearly drop the torch. I'm shaking. Somehow I manage to find the switch and shine the torch around. There's a girl lying on the mattress, looking up at me. She coughs. A coughing that shakes her whole body. So it was *her* that I heard from my bedroom.

She's trying to speak. 'Mother sent you, didn't she? I told Jimmy she would watch over us. You've come from Heaven to save us!'

I look around to check there's nobody else in the room. There isn't. She's talking to me!

'I'm just Ben. From next door,' I stammer. But she's sunk back on to the mattress, and closed her eyes. She looks really sick. I tiptoe over to her mattress and kneel on the floor. Her breathing sounds strange, sort of wheezy and hoarse. There's blood around her lips. She is paler than pale. 'What's your name?' I whisper.

'Mary,' she murmurs, and then she opens her eyes and smiles. 'I knew you'd come.'

'But Mary, I'm not an angel! I'm Ben. I live next door. I heard you coughing.' I give up trying to explain because she's fallen asleep. I sit there on the floor next to her bed for a minute or two trying to work out what is going on. And then I go off in search of the boy.

This time I manage to avoid the broken stair, and I get all the way down. I walk along the hall, and I notice that it seems less dusty and derelict than this afternoon. The front door isn't boarded up! I can see stained-glass flowers set into the wood, and next to the door are a little group of pictures. This is feeling very spooky indeed.

I make my way to the cupboard under the stairs. I push back the bolt and open the door. Crouched against the wall staring back at me is the boy. 'Jimmy?' I whisper cautiously.

'You know my name!'

'Mary told me.'

'Mary? Are you Mary's angel?'

'*No*! I'm just a normal boy!' He looks at me in my jeans and trainers like I'm anything but normal. 'How long have you been locked up in here?' I ask, trying to change the subject.

'Don't know. Lost track.'

'But I came back – with the police – and you weren't here.'

He looks terrified. 'No police! He'll kill us…'

'Who?'

'Father.'

'Your *dad* beats you up and locks you in this cupboard?'

'It's the drink. Gets him vicious. Worse now he's lost his job. Drinking all the time. Sold nearly every bit of furniture. Spends the money on more drink. Be nothing left soon…'

'What about Mary – does he hit her too?'

'You seen Mary?'

'I told you. Upstairs, on the bed.'

'Mary's going to … to die … because he won't pay for a doctor. And the twins aren't strong—'

'The twins?'

'Little Annie and Joe…' Jimmy is suddenly still. I soon realise why. The heavy step of his dad is thumping towards the cupboard door. I'm on the verge of leaping up towards my exit hole, when he passes by, and stamps up the stairs.

'Mary,' he yells. 'Shut that racket! Think we want to hear you coughing your guts up?'

Jimmy shrinks further into the shadows. We sit there listening to the shouting upstairs, not daring to move. Then, in the faintest of whispers, Jimmy speaks. I lean forward to try to catch his words. 'He didn't used to drink so much. Not when Mother was with us.'

'Your mum left, did she?'

'Our mother would never leave us! He killed her.' Jimmy spits out the words.

'Your dad *killed* your mother?'

'Good as.'

'What d'you mean?' I breathe, my mouth dry.

Jimmy sighs, staring ahead. 'Must be about a year ago now. Father – he's belting little Joey, and Mother – she tries to stop him. She was always trying to calm him. Anyway she's not very strong, and Father's built like an ox, so he pushes her out the way. Only she loses her balance and falls backwards down the stairs.'

'And that's what killed her?'

'No, she doesn't die straight away. She lies at the bottom of the stairs, moaning, "The baby's coming." So Mary, she runs up shouting, "The baby's not due for two months yet!" But the baby does start to come, and our father won't let us call the midwife in case she starts asking questions. So they both die, baby as well.'

I don't know what to say. Jimmy slumps back against the wall. Dead tired. Like he's just used up all his strength.

'Hey,' I hear my voice say. 'I'll think of some way out for you, Jimmy, I promise.'

He smiles weakly and whispers, 'Mary was right, wasn't she?'

Oh no, he's back on the angel stuff. I'm just about to put him straight when I realise he's shut his eyes. Very quietly I close the cupboard door behind me, and shine my faint torch beam up the stairs. I get to the landing without sticking my feet in any holes or making a single creak, and I'm just tiptoeing towards Mary's room, when the door opposite me swings open and I am face to face with … their *dad*!

Don't think I'd admit this to Amit, but I scream. He's a big man. Bigger than my dad! And he has an evil look: cold and hard. I'm so scared I can't move. Well, apart from shaking. And he just stands there, like he's thinking what to do with me. Then he opens his mouth and roars, 'Mary – I said shut up your coughing!'

He takes a step towards me, and another. He's on top of me. HELP! I shut my eyes. I open them. He's gone! Huh? I turn around and he's behind me, stomping into Mary's room.

He has … just … walked … right … through … me!

I'm still standing there, gobsmacked, when he comes out of Mary's room and is facing me again. This time as he moves towards me, I take a deep breath and look him straight in the eye. No response.

I croak, 'Cooee! Over here!'

Nothing!

Braver, I shout, 'Hey, Dogbreath! Come and get me!'

Absolutely no reaction! He really can't see or hear me!

WHOOSH! Aaargh, he's doing it again! He's just walked right through me, and gone back into his own room. That felt really weird!

My legs are like jelly, but somehow I get them to carry me into Mary's room. She's lying very still, but breathing, so I reckon she's sleeping. I hover over her, wondering if she's more solid than her father. I put my hand out to touch her.

And then I pull it back again. I can't bring myself to do it.

I climb back across the sills into my own room, put on my pyjamas, and get under the duvet...

•

I open my eyes and Mary is standing by my bed, pale and thin. I can see she's dying. And this awful look of disappointment fills her face. Disappointment in me. Then she starts whispering over and over, 'I thought you would save us... I thought you were our angel...'

I can't take it any more. I just start yelling, 'What could I do? How could I have helped?'

But she's not listening. She just keeps saying my name, 'Ben. Ben. Ben. Wake up, Ben!'

•

And it isn't Mary saying my name – it's Mum in her nightshirt, looking worried. 'Ben, you were shouting in your sleep. Are you OK?'

No, I am not OK. I am being haunted by a whole family of ghosts, as a matter of fact.

Mum is still waiting for me to answer.

'Do you believe in ghosts, Mum?' I say in the most offhand voice I can produce.

She ruffles my hair and says, 'Of course not, Ben. There's no such thing as ghosts! You've been reading those horror books again, haven't you? I'm always telling you they'll give you nightmares!'

Chapter Five

'Ben!'

'Get lost, Jack!'

'Martin's made bacon and eggs, and I'm having yours if you don't come!'

So I come. And I'm sitting there chewing, when I hear this big thud from next door. It's followed by a weak little whimper. I drop my fork and egg glops everywhere. 'Did you hear that?' I gasp.

'Of course I heard it, Ben. You're lucky the fork didn't smash the plate.'

'No, Mum! Before I dropped my fork. Didn't you hear anything?'

They're all looking at me again. In that concerned way.

'You're going bonkers, Ben!' says Jack, and Mum says, 'Be quiet, Jack,' very sharply.

I want to change the subject, but I can't let it drop. 'Do you know how long it is since anyone lived next door, Mum?' I ask.

'Ben, I do think you're getting—'

'I really need to know, Mum!' I say. 'We've been here five years and it's been empty all that time, hasn't it?'

'It looks like it's been empty for years and years,' says Martin. 'These Victorian houses need to be looked after, or they just rot.'

'There's old Mrs Rose across the road...' says Mum thoughtfully. 'I bet she's been here a while. She might be able to tell you something.'

Of course! She looks about a million.

'Can I go right now, Mum?'

'I don't see why not,' she sighs.

•

I ring the bell quickly before I can bottle out. I peer through the stained-glass flowers in the front door, and I can see the old lady coming slowly up the hall. When she finally opens the door she peers at me through her watery grey eyes, trying to work out what I'm doing there.

'Are you collecting for something?' she asks.

'Oh ... er ... sorry! No. Well, in a way. I'm trying to collect some facts actually. About the house next door to ours.' I turn and point to the boarded-up house.

'Oh, you mean number 37? That one's been empty for years. Now, if you don't mind, I can't stand awfully long these days, so if you want to talk I'll have to sit down.' And she starts walking slowly down the passage.

I shut the front door and follow her. She shoos a cat off an armchair before lowering herself into it, and I sit down on a matching one opposite.

It's weird being in this room, because its shape, its windows and fireplace are all in the same position as our living room, but hers feels so different. It's full of stuff: big dark furniture, yellowish patterned wallpaper, heavy net curtains. Every surface has got lacy mats covered with photos in frames.

She sees me looking round and says, 'My family!' She points to one of the photos, and I pick it up and bring it to her. It's a school photo of a kid with plaits. She kisses the picture in the frame. 'My darling little Ginny! She's my grandaughter, you know!' She looks across at me and I try to look interested. 'She's older now of course. About your age I should think. In her first year of secondary school.' I clear my throat, hoping to get her off this ultra-boring topic. She is undeterred. 'She'll be coming to stay for a few days when they break up for the holidays...'

I'm getting desperate. 'Who's this?' I say picking up an old brownish photo.

'My mother,' she smiles. 'She moved into this house when she was just a girl herself, and stayed here until she died. I've lived here most of my life, too. Goodness, have I seen some changes!' She stares at the photo and seems to go off into a dream.

'Has number 37 changed much, then?' I ask, hoping to get her back on the subject.

'Well … it's been a sad house as long as I've been here.'

'Have you known anyone who's lived in it?'

'Over the years a few families have moved in, and I've thought, "At last!" – but they've never stayed more than a couple of months. People say it's—'

'People say what?' I ask quickly.

She looks at me hard, through her milky eyes. 'Do you really want to know?'

'Yes,' I say.

'Well, people say that it's haunted: that terrible things went on there, and the spirits are trapped inside.' Her voice is very quiet, and I feel a shiver go down my spine.

'Mrs Rose, do you believe in ghosts?'

She doesn't laugh. 'The older I get, the less certain I am of things. And my mother always believed... But that's another story. There are many things we don't understand in this world.' She looks down and starts absent-mindedly stroking her cat. She's gone off into a dream again. I sit there for a while, and she suddenly looks up. 'I expect your mother will start wondering where you are if you stay any longer. But do come again. Perhaps when Ginny is here. You two could play in the garden!'

'Yeah...' (Yeah right!)

Chapter Six

I swing back through our gate, and a voice calls out, 'How did you get on?'

It's Smarmbin. He's crouched over our weedy flowerbed with a little fork and trowel.

'Fine,' I say, trying to walk past, but he's stood up, blocking my way. He's rubbing earth off his hands and grinning eerily at me.

'Your mother and I thought it would be really fun to go to the zoo today. Would you like that?'

'Great!' I say unenthusiastically. Actually I quite like the zoo, but I'd never admit that to him.

'Be ready to leave in about half an hour?'

I don't bother to answer, just make straight for my room and shut the door. I have things to think about.

Mrs Rose has provided me with a couple of very important facts: one – other people have heard and seen the kids next door, which means that two – I am not going mad. These keep me going for a couple of minutes.

But if these children are ghosts, that means they're already dead. In which case it must be too late to help them. So why do I have this nagging feeling that I *can* help them? You can't actually change history, can you?

There's just no one I can talk to about it. Mum's obviously out of the question. My mate Amit would assume I'd flipped out, and even old Mrs Rose would tell me there's nothing to be done.

Hey! There *is* something I can do! I jump up, and creep across the landing to the bathroom. As quietly as I can, I open the medicine cabinet. Great! There are plasters, antiseptic, and even cough mixture. I stuff them all under my T-shirt and rush back to my room. I empty out my school backpack, and put the medical stuff in the bottom. Then hide it under my bed.

Just in time.

'Ben, what a mess it is in here!'

'Oh, hi, Mum!'

'Can you tidy this lot up? We're leaving in a few minutes.'

•

Martin's Vauxhall isn't just boring, it's old. And he doesn't know how to look after a car like my dad does. My dad spends every Sunday washing and polishing and hoovering and tuning his car. Or he did. When he was here. Sometimes he let me help, but I wasn't much good at it. He'd always have to do my bits again. But that was three years ago. I bet I'd do it OK now.

I look at the rust on Martin's car, and shake

my head. Just like Dad would have done. Jack and me get in the back. We get stuck in millions of traffic jams, so it's lucky I've brought my Discman.

'I'm hungry! Can we stop and eat?' Jack's whining breaks through my Hardmachine track.

'We'll have our picnic when we get to the zoo,' says Mum.

Martin looks at his watch. 'Why don't you give the boys a sandwich to keep them going? It looks as though we'll be in the car for a while.'

We all look at Martin in disbelief. 'You don't mind us eating in the car?' Jack squeaks.

'Why should I mind?'

Dad would go mad if a stray toast crumb from your chin found its way into his car! No one would dare to suggest actually eating in it!

•

I am staring into the orang-utan cage. The big mother ape is looking back at me with sad orange eyes, and I'm thinking of Jimmy again … in his own cage … without a mother. I turn to look at my mum.

She's OK, my mum. Gets a bit naggy about us leaving stuff lying around, and doing homework and not watching telly all the time, but she's soft really. On a Sunday night we sometimes hire a DVD and get some popcorn, and switch off the lights and pull the telly up really near. Then we sit in a line, like we would in a cinema, but on the sofa, really close together: me, Mum and Jack. If the film's scary, we all scream. If it's funny, we all laugh...

Now Sunday nights will never be the same again. Martin'll always be there, sitting with Mum on the sofa, laughing in the wrong bits, eating all the popcorn... He'll probably choose all his favourite films without even asking us what we want, like Dad did. But at least Dad was our dad.

Blimey, I was miles away! The zoo's closing. Martin says we can get fish and chips on the way home. Mum slips her arm through his, and Jack grabs his other hand, and I trail behind the happy little family.

The fish and chips are quite good though.

We're home by six, and I'm just about to suggest a DVD when Mum mentions the 'h' word. Bum! I'd forgotten I still have to do my Biology. I grab a choccy biscuit, drag up to my room, and pull out my school bag. All the medical stuff I'd stashed there earlier falls out! I stare at it guiltily. I hadn't thought about the kids next door for most of the afternoon. I repack the bag, trying to work out what else would be useful in there.

By nine, I've done my homework, checked my e-mails, (nothing from Dad) and managed to sneak two packets of crisps, some cheese, four biscuits, and three apples out of the kitchen. I've also found two new torch-size batteries in the cutlery drawer. I've added all these to the medical supplies in my backpack. Not bad, eh?

At last it's time for bed!

I've brushed my teeth and I'm in my pyjamas in record time. Smarmbin wanders in and stands nervously by the door.

'Er – goodnight, Ben.'

'Night,' I say, pretending to read a book.

He gives a nervous cough. 'I just wanted to say that … that I really enjoyed today, and I … er … hope you did too?' He's willing me to be nice.

'Whatever,' I say, without looking up.

'See you in the morning then, Ben.'

Finally! He's gone.

Now it's Mum's turn. 'No nightmares tonight, then!' And she kisses me quickly before going downstairs to be with *him*.

I lie there silently for what seems like hours, but finally they go to bed. I put the new batteries in my torch, pull a sweatshirt and jeans over my pyjamas, put the backpack over my shoulders, and I'm off.

Chapter Seven

Mary is lying on her old rustling mattress, but she looks worse.

'Mary!' I whisper. 'I've brought you some cough mixture.' Her eyes flicker open but she isn't really awake. She's shivering, curled under a thin old blanket and some newspapers. I could have packed a hot-water bottle, but you don't think you'll be needing one in June.

Maybe it isn't June here. It does feel pretty cold and clammy. I reckon I'll give Mary the medicine later on, when she's awake, and go and see if Jimmy is around. I creep downstairs, carefully avoiding the broken stair. The little cupboard is bolted again. I quietly push the bolt across and go in. 'Jimmy!'

He looks up at me. God, he looks worse too – so thin and pale.

'Ben! I thought you'd forgotten us. It's been ages. Mary's dying, isn't she?'

'No! 'Course she's not. Anyway I've brought medicine. And look – here's food!' I hold out the crisps and fruit.

He looks at my hand. Then he shouts, 'Why are you mocking me? You know we're starving!'

'Take it then!' I shout back.

'There's nothing there. Your hands are empty.' He looks forlornly away.

I feel sick. I get out the plasters and cream. 'Can't you see this either?' I ask desperately.

His fierce look says it all.

And I thought I was finally going to be able to do something. I sink down next to Jimmy. 'Sorry,' I mumble.

We both sit there in silence for a while. Then Jimmy starts talking. 'What'll we do if Mary dies? She's been like a mother to us. And I've heard nothing out of the twins in days. Dunno what he's done with them.' Jimmy gazes blankly at the door, and I desperately rack my brains for an answer.

'Hey! What if you write a message for them? I could deliver it.'

Jimmy blinks up at me like I'm from another planet. 'We've never learnt writing. Mother, she always wanted us to learn. She said it's like magic when you know what those squiggles on the page mean, but we never...'

'Well, OK then.' I wish I'd kept my mouth shut, he looks like he might cry. 'Why don't I go and see if I can find Annie and Joe?'

Jimmy's face lights up, but I don't want to go. Mostly because I'm scared I might find them. Dead. I haven't heard a sound from them, not on any of my visits. But I get my torch out, sneak out of the cupboard and start creeping around.

The layout is just like home, only in reverse. I am in the sitting room (well, that's what it is in our house) and maybe it would have been here if there was anything to sit on! It's a dank, empty room with nothing in it but an old table, a broken wooden chair, and a cold stove against the wall.

Correction. It also contains Jimmy's dad! But he's slumped in a corner, his head rolling back against the peeling plaster. Maybe he's dead?

Suddenly he snorts, his mouth falls open, and a trail of dribble runs down his chin. I stand as still as a statue checking that there isn't anyone else I hadn't noticed. But there are definitely no children here, though there is a door in the corner of the room.

I tiptoe towards it. It has a key in the lock, which I carefully turn, and the door creaks open. It's pitch black on the other side. I click my torch on. Luckily. Or I would have fallen down a little wooden staircase. Of course, the cellar! We've got one too. To be absolutely truthful, I don't even like going down to our cellar. And this one looks like something Dracula would be proud of. But I remind myself that superheroes aren't scared of cellars and spiders and stuff. So I creak my way down the rickety wooden steps.

The first thing that hits me is the cold. The air feels sort of wet. The second thing that hits me is the stink. A bit like the nocturnal house at London Zoo. Animally.

I shine my torch around. The walls are all brownish with funny lumps on. Euch! They're mushroomy things! I back away into a pile of rotten old boxes. Yuk! They're all cold and slimy! I don't want to move any further into this horrible dungeon. I let the torch do the exploring. Its beam jumps around, picking out bits of broken glass, torn paper, empty old bottles … and then I see them.

Like a picture from one of my old fairytale books, *Babes in the Wood*. These two little kids, lying on the floor holding on to each other. Eyes closed. Only these two aren't rosy-cheeked and covered in leaves, with bluebirds tweeting around them. They're thin, and dirty and dressed in rags. White as white. Dead still.

I crouch down on the floor beside them, this tightness clogging up my throat. Some angel I turned out to be. Then there's a tiny, tiny movement … I think. I stare at them, willing it to happen again.

'Annie… Joe?' A flicker. 'Wake up. Come on! You must wake up!'

Annie stirs. Heavy eyelids half open. Then close again. 'Are we dead?' she murmurs.

'No, no, you're not dead! Please, please wake up. Jimmy and Mary need you!'

Annie's eyes open again. She groans, pulls herself up, looks around, confused, and then notices her brother on the floor next to her.

'Joe! Joey!' She begins frantically shaking her brother. 'Joey, wake up! You mustn't die. You promised me, remember? Joeeeey – we've got to find the others. Joe, pleeease wake up...' She rubs his hands, his cheeks, his skinny little arms – and I can hardly believe it, he starts to move!

'Annie!' His lips are blue but they open. Suddenly I want to put food in his mouth. Or water, or something. I know they can't see my food, let alone eat it, but maybe I can find them some food in their house.

I run up the wooden steps and creak open the cellar door. Ahead of me their dad is still slumped against the wall. He's not going to wake up in a hurry. This room leads off into the kitchen. I pray that I'll find something.

Yuk! What a mess! If Mum saw this she'd never complain about my room again! Dirty old dented pots and pans, filthy plates, flies buzzing all round the place, swarming in through the broken window. I look in the old stained sink for signs of something edible. Just peelings and dirty plates. The floor is littered with broken bits of china, rotting old vegetable ends and – hang on, an apple! A bit bruised and misshapen, but not too bad! I reach out to pick it up, and my hand slices through it.

My hand slices through everything. Each filthy pan is as thin as air. I spot a mouldy bit of bread lying in a corner on the floor, but my hand slips right past it. This is hopeless. Then I have an idea. Why didn't I think of it before? I'll unbolt Jimmy's door and *he* can get the food!

I race back towards the cupboard, unlock it and go in. 'It's OK! Annie and Joe are alive! But they need food and water. Can you help me take it to them?'

I hold the little cupboard door open for Jimmy. But he doesn't follow me out. He pulls further back into the shadows, eyes wide with terror. 'It's all right, Jimmy, your dad's snoring!'

But Jimmy shakes his head from side to side, 'Can't leave. He'll kill me. Got to stay. Can't go!' He's crouched in the corner, still with fear.

'OK, OK, Jimmy. It was just a thought. I'll find another way. Don't get upset. We're cool.'

'Freezing.'

I don't seem to be cheering him up much, so I say, 'See you in a while,' and head wearily for Mary's room. Maybe she can help.

But she looks terrible, lying there under the old newspapers. I squat down next to her mattress. I don't want to disturb her, so I just sit there, hypnotised by her crackling breathing. Mary twitches and my eyes refocus on the blurred bit of newsprint I've been staring at. And then I realise I've been gazing at a date: 4th April 1889.

Wow! That newspaper's well over a hundred years old! So this other world really is … is history! No wonder they talk so strangely. A hundred years... Man – this is a serious new piece of information.

But how does it help? I carry on sitting there in a sort of daze, trying to put this all together in my head. But my mind keeps drifting off.

Got to get some sleep! So I drag myself out on to the windowsill. Straddled between the two houses, I glance across the road at old Mrs Rose's house, and I get this weird impression of seeing a sun reflected in the glass. Then I nearly fall off the sill, because standing at one of the windows gazing back at me is a girl, looking as shocked as I feel. Has her grandaughter arrived already? I struggle to get my balance back, give her a shaky wave, and throw myself through my open window on to the bed.

The next thing I know, my mum is shaking me awake.

Chapter Eight

Oh no! Monday morning. School.

I tell you, those kids next door are getting to me. I am sitting at my desk doodling my signature on a piece of paper while Mr Fletcher hands out our Maths sheets, when I catch myself thinking that Jimmy would give anything to swap places with me. And I feel sort of guilty. And lucky...

Me, Ben Ryder, lucky? Nah! Hacked off, yes. But lucky – no way. I've got Smarmbin sat there in my dad's place, remember! Which reminds me that Dad never phoned or e-mailed the whole weekend. For a change.

Anyway, I've got more urgent things to worry about. Like saving an entire family. I have to think of some way to rescue them from that Neanderthal, and it has to be soon. Preferably tonight. So no pressure there, then.

But what can I do? I'm just a kid myself. What do I know? Nothing. No, not nothing. I know that they'll all die if I don't help them. I know the date – well, the date they're living in. It's around 1889. This has to help me. This has to be a clue.

A clue to what, damn it? What would the White Rider do?

Suddenly my tortured thoughts are interrupted by something even more unpleasant – Mr Fletcher's face two centimetres in front of mine. I have a feeling I've just failed to answer a question. Several times. Everyone waits. Someone sniggers. Mr Fletcher taps his fingers across my page of signatures. I am what you might call 'dead meat'.

Then Amit coughs, 'Twenty four,' under his breath.

'Twenty four?' I try, gazing innocently up at Mr Fletcher.

'Hmph,' he snorts, as he strides back to the front of the class. 'Next time, Benjamin Ryder, I'd like you to attempt an answer before I draw my pension.'

Phew! I owe you one, Amit.

I spend the rest of the day trying to concentrate on what I'm supposed to, but it's weird because it seems that every lesson reminds me of Jimmy. Like in History I work out that Victoria is the Queen of England in Jimmy's time. I wonder if he knows that...

Then in English, Mrs Gerard asks us to write about something really scary. And while Amit and Nick rabbit on about Body Snatchers and Terminators, all I can think about is how scary a dad can be.

It's a major relief when the bell rings and we can all go home. Of course, it's no easier when I get there because the noises through the walls have got louder than ever. Now it's not only Mary's hacking coughs I can hear, but their dad shouting and swearing, thundering up and down the stairs, slamming doors, hitting things. It's horrible. And Mum, Jack and Martin just carry on, chatting and laughing as though none of the thumping and whimpering is happening. Because for them, it isn't. They can't hear any of it. This must be how it feels to go mad, with voices locked in your head. I'm getting desperate.

I suddenly notice that I've got through half my dinner without even tasting it. And it's toad-in-the-hole – my favourite. Martin is droning on about work… Then something he says tunes me out of my own thoughts. 'Got to get the kids out of the home, they're not safe any more.'

It's like telepathy. He's just said what's been whirring around my brain. But he's not talking about Jimmy, Mary and the twins. He's talking about some social-work case he's been handed.

'Who takes kids away from bad parents?' I ask, hoping to get some useful information.

'Well…' says Martin, looking all flustered, 'Chil- children don't get taken away unless there's a really good reason.'

'But if there is?' I say, exasperated.

'Often the child thinks that the parents are bad, but really they aren't. Th- they're just doing their best.'

What is he going on about?

'…and I know it can be very hard for a boy who wants his own father back, to accept another man into the house…'

Oh, poor old Smartbin! He has the wrong end of the stick! Shall I put him out of his misery? Difficult. It's quite funny seeing him sweat, but I have a bit of schedule here, and I can't really waste time. 'Martin, I'm not talking about me!'

The relief on his face – I almost feel sorry for him. 'Actually, I'm really interested in finding out who would take kids away from bad parents a hundred years ago ... er ... for a project I'm doing at school.'

'Hmmm... Well...' Martin strokes his chin, 'There weren't social services as we know them a hundred years ago, so many children would have relied on a relation. And Barnardo only really helped homeless orphans. We can look through some of my books if you like, see if there were any other options?'

'Yeah, OK then.'

Martin beams at me, as though I'm doing *him* the favour, and after dinner we trot off to the back room where all his boxes of books are waiting to be unpacked.

I find out all sorts of interesting things about workhouses, and gas lamps, but I don't find out anything that's much use to Jimmy. In actual fact, I go up to my room feeling more on my own than ever.

Then I have to lie in bed doing my best to shut out the sound of Mary's weak coughing. It's like a hammer thumping out the message – *Time's running out... Time's running out...* I start to sweat, trying to sift through the information I've got. I have this niggling feeling that there's something useful I've missed.

I sit up and get a piece of paper and pencil. Got to be methodical. Now what do I know? OK, I know that the date is at least 1889. But what good does that do me? Barnardo has only just got going, and he only helps orphans. And though there are guys supposed to do stuff about horrible living conditions and getting kids to school, they're only just getting started, and it looks like they haven't spotted Jimmy's family. What was it Martin said? A hundred years ago children would have had to rely on a relative. Yeah, great. No mother and the dad from hell. Unless – unless there's somebody else. I mean, I've got Aunty Gemma (though you wouldn't wish her on anybody), and Granny and, come to think of it, there's Uncle Sam and his new girlfriend Lucy. So maybe...

My heart starts to beat really hard, like it's primed and ready for action. I listen at the door. I can hear Mum and Martin downstairs. I put out my light, stick my 'Anyone who Enters is Dead' notice on the bedroom door, and shove a pillow under my duvet. Not incredibly convincing, but good enough.

Chapter Nine

It's not dark yet and I'm just manoeuvring myself across the windows (which I'm getting pretty good at) when someone whispers, 'Hey, boy!'

Man, I nearly fall off the sill! Wobbling dangerously, I look down and, standing on the ground below me, hands on hips, is the girl I waved to from over the road last night.

My first instinct is to ignore her, and get on with my mission, but I soon realise that she isn't ignorable. She's talking again. 'Who are you? Are you a ghost? What are you doing up there?' She's getting shriller and shriller, and I'm sure someone will hear her. I have to shut her up. So I slide down the drainpipe – well, jerk down, actually, and when I finally get to the bottom, I realise immediately that I'm in Victorian time, because the parked cars and glass porches have disappeared. I am standing on a cobbled street opposite this girl who's wearing a long pinafore, which no girl would be seen dead in today.

'Hi!' I say, all casual. 'My name's Ben, what's yours?'

Now we're face to face she doesn't seem quite so sure of herself as she did. In fact she's gulping and looking seriously spooked. 'M-m-my name is … G-G-Georgina.'

I can't really think what to say to her, and I'm getting fidgety about the time and my mission. I'm also wondering if I really have to climb up the drainpipe again. Maybe I can get in the front door? So I mumble, 'See you around,' and edge towards Jimmy's door.

But would you believe it – this girl just can't take a hint, and she starts following me. 'What are you doing here?'

'Look – I haven't got much time,' I hiss back. 'Got to get going – er, nice to meet you, Georgina. Bye!'

She just stands there. I am losing my cool. 'What?' I say.

'You're not going into that house, are you?' She's really scared.

'Yeah, I am as it happens. So?'

'No one goes near that house. Bad things go on there… Screaming… Cursing…'

'You're telling me!' I snap. 'But it's not going to stop if nobody does anything.'

'Aren't you scared?' She's looking at me like I'm mad.

I think about it. 'Yeah, of course I am, but I suppose I'm mostly scared for the kids.'

'The kids?'

'The children – Jimmy, Mary and the little twins.'

'I didn't know there were children in there.'

'Haven't you ever seen them?'

She shakes her head. 'Once, I saw a lady standing at the window, holding a baby, but that was a long time ago.'

'Yeah? Well, she's dead now!'

'Dead? How did she die?'

'You don't want to know! Anyway, I'd better get going…' I move away from her. But she darts in front of me.

'What are you going to do?' She has her arms folded in front of her with this determined look on her face. And I don't really know why, but I suddenly just want to laugh. And then I find myself telling her everything. About Jimmy in the cupboard, and Mary coughing her guts out, and the twins in the cellar, and she just lets me talk until I've finished.

'So we need to find out whether they have a relation who can help them?'

'Yeah, that's what I thought…' I'm still mumbling, but I'm feeling this wave of relief, because she said 'we' and suddenly I don't feel so alone.

'Come on then,' she says, and I can tell she's trying to sound braver than she feels.

We move slowly towards the front door, but neither of us can get in. 'Can't you just waft through it, like you did with the upstairs window?' she asks, all annoyed.

'Apparently not!' I whisper crossly back, trying one more time to do just that. 'I can waft through some things,' I add a bit weakly. 'I wish I knew why!'

'Let's try round the back,' she says, striding towards the little alley between Jimmy's and the house on its other side.

The shabby wooden side-gate creaks as Georgina pushes through it. We freeze and wait, but nobody seems to react, so we creep into the dreary yard, which is filled with broken bits of furniture.

'Pheeoww!' Georgina holds her nose. 'What a stench!' and she points to this little outhouse.

I can't smell anything at all.

'The privy!' she says, gasping for air.

I peek in. Yuk! It's a toilet! And it is beyond disgusting.

'Look!' Georgina is pointing towards the broken kitchen window. 'We could get through there.'

She's right. There's no glass, just a plank of wood leaning against it. She moves the plank and climbs through. I follow. And bounce back into the yard.

What is going on? I try again, and just can't get through. She's standing inside the kitchen looking terrified, her courage is on the verge of failing.

'Try opening the back door,' I whisper.

Her eyes dart right and left, to check no one is coming and then she slowly turns the key. Once the door opens I slip in, and she shuts it behind me.

This is so weird, coming through the house from a different angle. I take the lead, and Georgina stays in the shadows behind me. I check the dining room for their dad. He doesn't seem to be there, so I wave her through.

We're in the hall, by the cupboard.

'Jimmy, are you in there?' I whisper.

'Ben? Is that you?'

Slowly, careful not to make a sound, Georgina unlocks the bolt, and we squeeze inside.

Jimmy starts back at the sight of Georgina, but I tell him she's OK, she's here to help. I turn to Georgina for confirmation, but she isn't looking exactly helpful. In fact she's swaying and holding on to the door frame. I suppose I should have warned her about Jimmy. He's looking pretty bad; more bruised and swollen than ever, with patches of dried blood, and grimy scabs covering his skinny little body. Georgina can't hide her shock. It's a tricky moment, so I start talking fast.

'Jimmy, do you have any relatives apart from your dad? Somewhere else you could go? Someone who could take care of you all?'

He's looking bewildered, poor kid. Just sits there looking blank. I give him a moment, and try again. 'Do you have any grandparents – or aunties – or anyone?'

He shuts his eyes and starts rocking backwards and forwards. I look sideways at Georgina, whose eyes are wide, her fists clenched.

Then Jimmy starts to mutter. 'Mother, she was always talking about our grandmother, how much she would love us if she knew us. I think Mary was took there once, in secret. But Grandmama's never come here. Nobody comes here. He wouldn't have it. He hit Mother if he heard her talking about her own family. "We're yer family now, and don't you forget it!"'

'What is your grandmother's name?' whispers Georgina.

'Dunno. Just Grandmama.'

'Jimmy, d'you think Mary would know?'

Jimmy's eyes refocus. 'I don't know if Mary is still l-living. I haven't heard her coughing...'

I feel icy. 'I'll go upstairs and find out. Georgina, are you staying or coming?'

'I think I'd better come with you. Er ... see you soon, Jimmy.'

'I'll be back, Jimmy. Just hold on.'

Georgina and I creep carefully up the stairs. She has to be careful not to creak. I have to be careful not to fall down any holes – which don't seem to be there for her. When we get to the top, we hear Mary's weak little cough, and I breathe a sigh of relief.

But it is followed by another sound. A deep rumbling, coming from one of the other rooms. Georgina's eyes widen. The door is ajar so I stick my head round. It's their dad lying across the bed with his boots still on. Snoring. Out cold. Phew.

Georgina is holding on to the banisters with white knuckles. I whisper the good news, and we tiptoe into Mary's room. Poor old Georgina, her face turns another shade whiter when she sees the ragged, barely conscious girl huddled under newspapers in the corner.

'Mary!' I say in a low voice. Her eyes flicker, but don't open. Her hand moves slightly. 'Mary, we have to find your grandmother, so she can look after you, and make you better.' I pause, hoping she can hear me. Her heavy eyes open just a bit, and her dry cracked lips try to smile.

'Do you know her name, or where she lives? Mary?' It's like she's drifting away. 'Mary!'

She drifts back to me. 'Same name as Mother. Emily. Emily Jackson. Emily and ... Thomas Jackson.'

'Is Thomas your grandfather?'

Mary nods, and closes her eyes.

'You don't know where they live, do you?'

'Long way. Had to get the tram ... and the train ... trees and fields ... lovely ... only saw them once...'

'Mary, can you remember an addr—'

There is a huge thump and we all jump. It's coming from the bedroom next door.

'Mary! Whatime zit? You still in bed, yer lazy skiver?' Their dad is coming in and we have to get out. If he catches Georgina...

'Quick, through the window!' I croak. Georgina, shaking, starts stumbling through. 'Just get to the windowsill next door, and hold on!'

Their dad staggers in the doorway, and Georgina's shoulder and hand are still on this side of the window. He raises his head and his eyes travel round the place, but he is so drunk, he just stands there swaying and frowning. By the time his eyes focus, Georgina is gone, and I'm not far behind!

We both wobble on the windowsill outside my bedroom, clinging on to the frame for support. 'D'you think you can make it down the drainpipe?' I ask.

'You managed.'

'Listen,' I say urgently. 'Would you be able to—'

'Find out anything about Emily and Thomas Jackson? I'll do my best. Our maid might know something – she likes to gossip!'

'There's something else...' I hesitate. Am I pushing my luck? Ah well, nothing ventured... 'You know the children are starving?'

'Yes, I'm sure I can sneak some food from the larder without too much trouble. But I'd rather not have to take it over to them alone...' She shudders, and I want to give her a little pat, but I can't let go of the window frame.

'Thanks, Georgina! Of course we'll do it together – tomorrow night, same time?'

She looks at me blankly. 'But it's daytime – I'll be late for luncheon if I don't hurry!'

I look from her to the street, and I get this weird dizzy feeling. It is definitely dark now – I can see the moon and a smattering of stars – but when I stare I can also see a faintly shimmering sun! The windows of Georgina's house are both open and shut, like one of those 3-D pictures that look different at different angles. It's making me feel a bit sick, so I say, 'You'd better get going! I'll see you as soon as I can. Night!'

She rolls her eyes, grins, and gives a nervous look around. The coast looks clear so she starts gingerly down the drainpipe. I'm impressed. It's not easy to do in jeans, but in a stupid dress and petticoats it must be twice as hard. Well, I suppose she doesn't have a lot of choice, but I'm impressed anyway.

At last she reaches the ground, and waves. But as she crosses the road, she just sort of fades away. I stare into the empty street, willing her to reappear. But it's as if she were never there.

I am shivering. I climb back through my window, get into bed, shut my eyes and try to think happy thoughts.

Chapter Ten

Seconds later (it seems) Mum is shaking me out of a very pleasant dream, and I am not happy. She stomps out of my room, calling behind her, 'Fine! Stay in bed – but in ten minutes you'll have missed the school bus.'

I groan. Back to the real world. School. Urgh!

But as I get into my uniform, I'm feeling better than I have for ages. Can't think why really. OK, I'm lying. I'll admit it's because of Georgina. Now I've got someone to share all this stuff with. A friend. But it's stupid, because she isn't even real, and she probably won't be there again. This thought makes me feel a bit panicky, so I push it away, run downstairs, grab a couple of custard creams, pick up my school bag and head for the bus.

'Ben!' Mum is shouting from the front door. I stop and turn. 'Have a nice day at school, love!' I give her a wave and run on.

•

I manage to get through double History and French without too much trouble, and then it's only one lesson until dinner – Geography. Brilliant! Ha! Got you! Brilliant because Miss

Wilmott never looks up from her notes. And this gives a person plenty of thinking time.

Which I use.

I think about my new friend, Georgina. And what an advantage it is to have a friend in the right time zone, who can maybe get hold of real food that can be touched and eaten! Unlike me and my invisible offerings.

And that's when it hits me!

I can touch stuff that exists in their time and mine, like the house. The house is as solid for me as it is for them. But an old apple would have rotted away years ago, so it couldn't be solid for me now! Yeah, and the stuff I brought for Jimmy, that he couldn't see, well, crisps hadn't even been invented then, so it was no wonder he couldn't see them, let alone eat them!

I sit there very pleased with myself for some minutes, checking through all the facts that make my theory work: the hole in the cupboard ceiling that Jimmy can't see, the way I can waft through some things and not others. It all makes sort of sense! Before I can catch myself out with a bit that doesn't add up, I move on to another thought: our new lead – the grandparents. Wouldn't it be brilliant if they were a way out for the kids!

But finding them may not be easy. Jackson isn't the most unusual name in the world, and I shouldn't think a letter addressed to Emily and Thomas Jackson, The Countryside, would have much hope of reaching them, even in Victorian time. And as all the finding out can only be done by Georgina, I end up trudging out of the Geography room at lunchtime feeling pretty helpless.

The rest of the day speeds past as we have double Art (cool) and Biology, which I can't help being interested in, so before I have any more time to brood I am turning my key in the lock of our front door.

Bum! Martin is back from work early.

'Hi, Ben!' he calls all bright and perky from the kitchen.

'Hey,' I mutter back.

'Fancy a cup of tea? I'm just making some.'

'Yeah, OK.'

'I've been doing a bit more research,' he says, this big grin all over his face.

I stare back at him blankly.

'You know, for your school project...'

'School project?' I'm lost.

'The Victorians. You know, the children you were asking about?'

'Oh, yeah – the children!'

'Anyway, I found out that the NSPCC had been set up by then...'

'So?' This doesn't mean much to me.

'So – the children could be reported to them, and in some cases taken away from bad parents!'

'Wow!' This is good news! Seriously good news!

'Trouble is, in 1889 the organisation was still pretty small, and I don't know how powerful it was, but in principle they could authorise removal! Not bad, eh?'

'Not bad!' I answer, and I just can't help grinning back at him. Can't wait to tell Georgina.

•

If you'd told me a month ago that I could spend a whole evening willing it to be time for bed, I would have laughed in your face! But I'm not laughing now. I'm jiggling and twitching, and drumming and fidgeting. The clock hands have just given up moving.

'I'm off for a bath,' I say as casually as I can.

My mum can't hide her shock. 'Are you all right, Ben?'

If I wasn't so desperate to get upstairs I would have been offended. 'Yeah, sure. Night, everyone!'

'But it's only eight o'clock!'

'A bit tired,' I mutter and dash off.

Chapter Eleven

When the coast is definitely clear I open my window and lean out. It's still incredibly light. Normal street, cars, pavement, tarmac. No sign of curious neighbours. And no sign of Georgina. I get a surge of panic, but try to ignore it as I climb across the sills. Before going through Mary's window I hang about on the sill scanning the street again.

Still no Georgina. My stomach starts to churn. I tell myself that she'll turn up, and after all, the day before yesterday she didn't even exist for me, so I can just carry on without her.

But I can't get anywhere without her, the panicky part of me answers.

I force myself to climb into Mary's bedroom. Once inside, I take one more unrewarding look at the street, and turn towards Mary's mattress.

Mary isn't there! I feel sick. Mary is always there! I check around the room for clues. The only certain thing is that I am back in Victorian time, because the old newspaper is there, and so is Mary's thin, threadbare blanket.

I hold my breath, fearing the worst, and creep towards the stairs. As I pass their dad's bedroom

I stop to listen. Can't hear anything so I peer round the door. What a pit! But it's an empty pit.

Careful to avoid the loose floorboards, I creak downstairs. My heart is pounding so hard that I don't immediately hear what's going on. It's not until I am almost on top of them that I realise.

All the children are sitting on the floor of the dining room whispering to each other, giggling and ... eating! And sitting with them is Georgina! Fear makes them all jump when they catch sight of me, but as soon as they realise it's not their dad they start grinning happily. Even Mary looks stronger.

Jimmy pulls himself up. 'Ben! We thought you would never come back!'

'B-b-but I was here yesterday!'

'Yesterday!' snorts Georgina. 'I waited every day for two weeks! In the end I became so worried I had to act alone!'

I stand there totally confused.

'Georgina's been so brave!' says Mary admiringly.

Huh! Georgina's only been around five minutes and already she's the hero.

'I've not really been brave, Mary,' corrects Georgina. 'I've just been thorough. I watched the house, and simply found out that your father leaves every evening...'

'...to go out drinking,' Mary sighs.

'And he's always gone for ages, so I thought it would be reasonably safe to sneak in after that.'

'And she keeps bringing us all these things to eat,' pipes up Joe, spattering bits of meat pie all over the place, and waving at a fast-disappearing pile of bread, apples, fruit cake and cheese.

Everyone looks so happy I'd have to be made of stone not to be pleased. Good old Georgina. And to be honest, she has been brave – we both know that if Jimmy's dad had caught her here, she'd be dead.

'So how many times have you been in?' I ask.

'This must be the fifth or sixth!' Georgina smiles proudly. 'See how much better Mary's looking! She couldn't get out of bed at first.'

Mary is certainly looking better. She's leaning on Jimmy, but she is smiling.

'And Jimmy,' I whisper under my breath, as we move out of earshot, towards the fireplace. 'You got Jimmy out of the cupboard!'

Georgina's face is serious. 'It wasn't easy, he was so afraid. And so bent over. He couldn't stand upright. Still can't really.' I glance across at the crouching figure on the floor. 'But I'm hoping, with time—'

'Time is the one thing we don't have.'

'I know, I know!' Georgina moans, her eyes darting nervously towards the front door.

'Have you managed to find out anything

about the grandparents?'

'I've found out some details, but nothing very useful.'

'Like what?'

'Well, that horrible drunken monster has a name – James Barker – and when he met their mother, Emily, he was an apprentice wool trader. How she could have fallen for him, or got her father's consent to marry him, I can't imagine, for Molly says that Squire Jackson was a well-respected gentleman farmer and landowner.'

I look around the filthy, decaying room and shake my head. 'None of this makes sense. How could they let their daughter live like this? Didn't they ever come and visit her?'

'Molly says she's never seen visitors.'

'But Emily took Mary to see them, remember?'

Georgina shrugs. 'Maybe Emily didn't tell them about her life.'

'So they may not even know that Emily's dead!'

'Possibly. But they may be dead themselves.'

'Oh don't say that, Georgina. They're our best hope.'

'They're our *only* hope.'

'Does Molly know the address of the Jacksons' farm? We have to contact them.'

'Molly couldn't tell me. Oh – Mary! Mary, I'm

sorry, don't weep.' Too late we see that Mary has edged closer, and has heard everything.

She is breathing hard, her face twisting with misery. 'Poor mother,' she whispers, and her hand touches a chain at her neck.

'What's that, Mary?' Georgina asks gently.

'It's mother's locket – she made me take it when she was dying. She said, "Don't let your father pawn this, Mary, keep it safe…"' Mary begins to sob. 'She t-t-took it out of her b-b-box and k-k-kissed it. I have to wear it hidden, see, so he never catches sight of it.'

'Does it open, Mary?' says Georgina. 'Can I see inside?'

But Mary has gone stiff. Her eyes widen, and she whispers urgently, 'He's back!'

The room goes sickly quiet, as we hear the heavy step at the front door. Jimmy dashes to his place under the stairs, the twins practically fall down the steps to the cellar, and Mary tries desperately to clear up the food.

'Georgina, get out!' I croak, as she starts to help Mary. Georgina suddenly realises the danger she's in and runs to push up the kitchen window. I hear her crash to the ground outside as the front door thumps open.

Chapter Twelve

Thud thud thud. James Barker's heavy steps make their way unsteadily towards us. I feel sick as his enormous shape fills the doorway. He sways and looks blearily around the room, then he sees Mary, cowering against the wall.

His expression becomes focused and vicious. 'Oh, so little poorly Mary's not at death's door then? She's been shamming all these weeks, has she?' He lunges towards her and she steps sideways to avoid him.

'Too sick to clear up this pigsty, but well enough to dance about the house when my back's turned? Eh?' This time he lunges and doesn't miss. His fist makes contact with her jaw, and the force of it knocks her to the ground. Two apples she's been hiding behind her back bounce out of her hands and roll noisily across the floor.

'So,' snarls James Barker, 'a ... liar ... and ... a ... thief!' With each word he kicks her thin little body, which crumples silently under his boot.

'Stop it! Stop it!' I yell, but he can't hear me.

'Where d'yer get the apples, girl?' he spits, but Mary doesn't answer.

I rush at him, but I am like air, and make no impact.

'Father,' she whimpers, her hands across her face, her shoulders hunched around her ears, but he doesn't stop kicking.

'He's going to kill her,' I moan. 'He's going to kill her.'

And then the miracle happens. There is a loud hammering at the front door. James Barker turns slowly, and listens. The knocking continues. He stands there, swaying slightly, then takes a couple of staggering steps towards it.

'Maybe it's the NSPCC?' I think, well – pray, actually. Then he takes a few more steps down the hall.

'What d'yer want?' he shouts.

The hammering continues. I squeeze past him to get a glimpse of who's out there. I peer through a piece of clear glass in the doorframe. It isn't the NSPCC. It's Georgina, hammering her fists off.

And James Barker's heading straight for the door! I wave frantically at Georgina through the glass. She sees me, nods, but carries on! I hope she knows what she's doing. I head back to the dining room.

I kneel down by Mary. She's got blood oozing from her mouth, and she's groaning. She's trying to speak. 'Mother's box...' she gasps, painfully raising an arm to point towards the window. Must be delirious.

'Mary, that's just a window...'

But she won't let it go. 'Up there,' she croaks. 'Above... You must get it...' She's pointing to a pelmet thing above the window, a sort of ledge.

'OK, Mary, I'll get it, don't worry,' I say, but I'm not really thinking about the box. I am thinking how I can get Mary out of this place tonight.

'Promise me,' she whispers, her eyes pleading.

'What? Promise you what?' I am so distracted I can't think straight.

'Promise you'll ... get ... the box.'

'Yeah, yeah, I promise,' I say, but I am listening to what's going on in the hall. James Barker has just opened the front door and he's yelling on the doorstep, 'Whaddyer want? Come back here, and I'll give you what for!' Now he's lumbering down the front path.

'Mary, can you move?' Mary tries to raise herself on one elbow and then collapses down again. I can't help her, so I shout to the others. Jimmy creeps out from under the stairs, and the twins come up from the cellar. 'You've got to get out of here!' I say.

But Jimmy frowns and spits, 'We're not going to the workhouse. Here, Mary, I'll help you upstairs.'

I watch, helpless, as they make their painful way up to Mary's filthy mattress. The twins, who have been keeping watch at the front door, suddenly squeak, 'He's coming back – quick!' They dart down to the cellar, picking up the apples on the way, Jimmy slips back down the stairs and into the cupboard, and I hang around in the empty dining room.

The door slams shut again, and all the windows rattle. What's he going to do when he sees Mary's not where he left her? I am shaking.

James Barker stumbles down the hall into the dining room. I have to suppress all my instincts to run. He stands in the doorway, scratching his head, and then he makes for the stairs. I want to be sick, but I follow him up. I can't leave. When he gets to the top of the stairs, he sways a bit, and then staggers towards his own bedroom where he collapses on to his bed. He starts to snore almost straight away.

I suddenly realise I haven't taken a breath for ages. I take a few deep ones, and then go to see how Mary's doing. She looks like an injured bird lying there on the mattress. 'Mary?' I whisper.

She opens her eyes and tries to smile, 'Our guardian angel...' She closes her eyes again.

Yeah! Some guardian angel! What have I managed to guard her from? Nothing. I am about as much use to Mary as—

'Mother's box... Must get it...' Mary suddenly gasps urgently, and I remember my promise.

But I won't be able to get it anyway. Even if there really is a box behind the pelmet, my hands will just slice through it, like they did through the food. On the other hand, at least I can see if it's there, then maybe I can get Georgina to climb up and get it.

The decision has been made, and however pointless, at least I'll be doing something.

The dining room seems more shadowy and ominous than ever. I have to climb on to the windowsill and then up on to the narrow wooden cross-frame. This is not easy, even for an ace climber like me. There is nothing very much to grip on to, and my feet can't stabilise. I start to fall and grab for the pelmet, expecting my hands to slip through. But it's solid! It's supporting my weight, and I am easing myself along the width of the window, feeling behind it with my fingertips. Suddenly my hand brushes against something smooth and hard. I stop moving and let my hand explore the shape. It is definitely a box. A wooden box! My hand curls round it, and I grab it. I jump down from the sill, and dash upstairs to Mary.

She's asleep, and cannot be woken. Should I leave the box here next to her, or will her dad find it? The thought of how he'd react if he found her with this box makes my stomach heave. I'll take it with me, and bring it back tomorrow. But as I climb back into my own room with the box under my arm, the awful thought occurs to me that my tomorrow could be a lifetime away for Mary, a lifetime she doesn't have.

Chapter Thirteen

I sit for a few moments on my bed, waiting for my heartbeat to slow down to something like normal. I put my bedside lamp on and examine Mary's box. It's filthy, so I take a corner of my pillow and wipe the muck off. It makes you cough, all that dust. But it's amazing what it's hiding! The box is made of really dark wood, with pictures of birds, flowers and leaves cut in to it with other lighter, different-coloured woods. It must have taken ages to make. I run my fingers over it, and however slowly I go, I can't feel any ridges, it's completely smooth!

I'm on the verge of opening it, when I nearly jump out of my skin. Someone's calling my name. Bum! Mum must have heard me come back. I shove the box under the bed. And hurl myself under the covers. But it's not Mum. The voice is coming from outside.

Nervously I go over to the window, and … I nearly scream. Georgina is standing on the sill peering in! She nearly jumps out of her skin when she sees me too! I open my window.

'Ben, thank goodness I've found you! I don't know what to do! I think James Barker has finally done for Mary. She's barely in this world any more…'

Again I am bewildered. I only left Mary a few moments ago, and Georgina was nowhere to be seen…

I stare at Georgina's face, and I'm struck by how different she looks. A couple of nights ago, when we first met, she was one of those happy, confident, smiley kids, without a care in the world. Now she looks pinched and desperate. She sits down on my windowsill, her feet dangling against the outside brick, and begins to cry.

I sit down next to her, and try to put my arm round her, but her shoulders are no more solid than air.

'M-Mary doesn't seem to know any of us any more. She talks only about her angel, whatever that means, and her mother, and – I don't know, something about a box … her mother's box.'

'I have the box!' I step back in to the room to get it. When I perch back on the window ledge, Georgina is wiping her face with a lacy handkerchief.

She gasps and almost loses her balance when she touches the box, and it is as solid for her as i   r me. This is a really awesome moment. – Georgina and me sitting on the sill there, unable to touch each other, but completely connected by this box that we can both hold.

'Is this really Mary's box?' she whispers, running a finger over the surface. 'It's so beautiful. We'd better take it to her – come on!'

We are kneeling by Mary's mattress. She looks terrible. Her face is swollen with cuts and bruises, and her lips are dry and cracked. Georgina is gently trying to wake her, but Mary's laboured breathing doesn't change.

I try. 'Mary, I've found your mother's box. Here...' I put the box beside her, and move her hand so she can feel it. Her fingers move; then her lips move. Her eyes open a little and she sees us, and then she sees the box. But she is so weak, she can do no more.

'Shall I open the box for you, Mary?' asks Georgina.

Mary nods.

Before she opens the box though, Georgina fishes a piece of candle out of her pinafore pocket, and strikes a match across the floor to light it. She balances it on the floor, so the box is in its own little spotlight. The lid is a bit stiff, but Georgina gets it open, and a sort of lavender scent fills the air.

Mary gasps, and sobs, 'Mother...' and Georgina's hands start to shake.

There are no jewels or coins in the box, just folded yellowish papers tied with a piece of blue velvet ribbon. Georgina carefully takes the package out, unties the ribbon, and gently unfolds the sheets of paper.

'This is a letter,' she whispers as she looks at the first sheet. 'Mary, these are letters from your grandparents – look!'

Mary opens her eyes again, but shakes her head. 'Can't ... read...' she coughs.

Georgina offers her some sips of water from a chipped old cup, while I, dying to see these letters, lean across to get a glimpse.

At the top left-hand corner of the first page is an address. Well, not just *an* address – *the* address! The one we've been desperate to find out! I point it out to Georgina, she nods back at me, and we share a moment of such brilliant excitement, it is all I can do to stop myself jumping around the room and yelling!

Georgina is more controlled. 'Would you like me to read the letters to you, Mary?' Mary barely nods, but her fingers tighten on Georgina's dress, and Georgina starts to read.

Deepcote Farm
Fallowhill
Berkshire

2nd March 1875

Dearest Emily,

It seems a lifetime since you left, and your father and I have had many long evenings to consider your unexpected departure and marriage.

We now believe that perhaps we were harder on you and more dismissive of James than was appropriate. Indeed, I now feel it was very wrong of us to refuse to attend your wedding. But it is a great comfort knowing that even without a dowry you are well provided for.

I know your husband James remains angry, and refuses to see us, but I hope you will find it in your heart to forgive us. We so long to see you and the new baby, our little grandaughter.

Do send us word or, better still, come and visit,
With fondest love,
Mother

The letter looks very creased and smudged, and I picture Mary's mother reading it over and over.

There are other letters, with later dates, and it becomes clearer and clearer that Emily's parents knew nothing of her wretched life.

16th September 1884

Dearest Emily,

What joy: Twins! How happy you must be!
James must be the proudest of husbands and fathers.

I am so glad that the servants and nanny are
keeping you from over-tiring yourself, for
confinement is very exhausting, and your health is so
precious. I am pleased to hear what a devoted father
James is proving, and we can perfectly understand
that he cannot bear to part with his children even for
the one day it would take you to visit us. But do try
to prevail upon him, for we do so long to see our
grandchildren. My love to you always.

Please kiss all your little ones for me,
Mother

I feel like bursting by the end of this letter.
'Servants! Nanny! But we know she didn't have
anyone to help her! Why did she tell her parents
such rubbish? Why couldn't she tell them what
was going on and go home?'

Georgina looks at me like I'm mad. 'Ben,
Emily was a married woman, she could not
return to her parents!'

'Why on earth not?'

'Well, it would be a scandal! She would be
disgraced, and her parents utterly shamed.'

'Oh, come on, Georgina, you can't be serious! None of it was her fault!'

'She *married* him!' Georgina splutters, shaking with exasperation. 'And without her parents' blessing! There would have been little point in telling them what her life was really like because nothing could have been done.'

What is she on about? 'Of course it could have! He should have been locked up years ago. You can't go around hitting your wife and children!'

'He was her husband!'

'And our father,' sighs Mary.

'Yeah but—'

'Sshh!' Mary stiffens. James Barker, the man who has caused all this misery, is stirring from his drunken stupor. 'You must get out,' she murmurs.

You're telling me! We are already half-way through the window.

'Take the box!' she croaks.

'You get out, Georgina, I'll get it!' I hiss.

Georgina gratefully accepts the suggestion and I see her heels disappear just in time. I'm dashing for the window, with the box in my hands when I hear this almighty bellow behind me. Then his great arm swings right through me, as his hand reaches for the box I'm clutching! Oh no! He can't see me, but he can see the box! It must look so weird floating around in front of him. I dodge and he misses, but he's grabbing for it again. I climb all round the room trying to escape him but his frustration is making him more accurate, and his swipes are getting vicious. I can't hold on much longer, and I can't let him get the box.

I make a break for the window and see Georgina clinging on to the drainpipe. I dart quickly away. Can't lead him straight to her. I'll have to head for the stairs.

I am clattering down two steps at a time, his heavy weight thundering behind me. I am in such a state I forget the broken stair, and suddenly I'm crashing through the rotten floorboards, into the cupboard below. I land exactly as I did on that very first day, in a crumpled heap on Jimmy's rag-bed, just missing his crouching body. And I am still holding the box.

Jimmy's dad has stopped chasing me. I guess he can't see the broken stair, so as far as he's concerned the box has just disappeared! It would make me laugh if I wasn't so scared. He starts shouting and swearing and smashing his fist into the wall, while Jimmy and I crouch shivering in the cupboard just below him. Then his heavy feet stomp all the way down the stairs, and we stiffen like statues. Jimmy grabs the box and shoves it under the rags, and we hold our breath.

The steps are coming towards us. The door splinters as Jimmy's dad kicks it. But the lock doesn't turn. There is silence for a few seconds and then mumbling. 'Need to get out. Stinking hellhole. Gotta find a drink…' and he's heading for the front door.

I pray Georgina hasn't climbed down yet, as he opens the front door and slams out.

'I'd better get going, Jimmy,' I whisper.

'Here, take it!' says Jimmy, handing me the box. We both hold on to it for a second, sharing it, and then I take it, climb through the hole above me, and go up to Mary's room.

When I get on to the sill, to my great relief Georgina is still there. She points towards the disappearing figure of James Barker.

'Georgina, you must take the box!'

'I know. I was waiting.' She takes the box and makes a sling for it in her pinafore. Just before she starts her awkward climb down the drainpipe, she adds, 'I'll send the letter within the hour!'

Chapter Fourteen

It's Friday morning: double Maths, double Physics and Biology. And I don't care! We've found the Jacksons! Georgina may have already written to them! It's like we got past the Dragon and found the Treasure! Or whatever! Nothing can get to me today. Nothing! Nothing, that is, until Mrs Shah the Biology teacher walks in, carrying a wad of papers under her arm.

Oh no! The test! The test I haven't revised for. The test I had forgotten all about. I can't even remember what it's on. 'Bacteria,' whispers Amit darkly. Oh yeah! And I'd been quite interested in them in the lesson, especially when Mrs Shah grew a *Streptococcus* in a dish. That was cool. But this isn't. She's handing out the papers and I am feeling sick.

'You may begin,' says Mrs Shah from the front of the class. I look at the paper and can't remember the name of anything except *Streptococcus*. I write it in four boxes hoping that one of them will be right, and glance hopelessly through the rest of the paper. I'll get one per cent if I'm lucky. Then I see a question with a huge blank space for the answer.

Write about any one of the bacteria we have been looking at. Describe its shape, its favoured breeding conditions, and the symptoms it produces. How would the symptoms be treated?

I sit there rolling my pen across the desk willing the fire alarm to ring. It doesn't. The only sound in the room is the urgent writing of all the people who *have* revised for the test. I start trying to think back to the lessons, and then suddenly out of nowhere something comes back. *B-bacillus*. Yeah! *Tubercle bacillus*. I write it down quickly before it goes again. And then it's like a tap I just switched on. I can remember it all! I remember the stick-like shape, because I drew a diagram, and I remember that it is spread by coughing. How it's more likely to spread in poor living conditions, and how it damages the lungs and … and… God! Suddenly I feel cold.

Mary's got it! Mary's got tuberculosis. She's got all the symptoms. Loads of people used to die of it, Mrs Shah said, before we had antibiotics.

I sit there numb until the bell goes. In fact I don't even notice it *has* gone. I don't notice anything until the vague nothingness in front of me is suddenly replaced by Mrs Shah's face. How long has she been standing over my desk?

'Ah, Benjamin – good of you to join me.'

'Sorry, Mrs Shah…'

'Is it a problem with revision, bacteria or something quite unrelated?'

I can't think what to tell her, and then figure I've got nothing left to lose, 'Er … Mrs Shah, were there antibiotics in 1889?'

She gives me one of her exasperated looks, 'Benjamin, do you sleep through all my lessons? Antiobiotics didn't become available for another fifty years. Does the Second World War ring any bells?'

My heart sinks. 'So if a kid my age got tuberculosis in 1889, would … would she die?'

'Not necessarily. It would depend on living conditions and how much damage the bacteria had caused. Remember the diagrams? The *bacillus* usually begins by attacking the lungs, but can then go on to spread its damage to other organs. This is why the Victorians called it consumption: they saw it as a disease that "consumed" the body.'

I picture Mary lying there on that filthy mattress, covered by old rags and newspapers, being consumed by the disease. But Mrs Shah said that people didn't always die. So maybe we can save her! Yeah, right! No antibiotics, no decent food, a father who beats her senseless. It's hopeless. I bury my face in my hands.

'Benjamin,' Mrs Shah's voice reminds me where I am. 'I'm very pleased that you are beginning to take such an active interest in biology – but even the best scientists need to take a break and get lunch, and we are no exception. Come along.' She pushes me towards the dining hall and locks up the lab.

Chapter Fifteen

I spend the whole of double French avoiding all thoughts of consumption. I also manage to avoid all thoughts of French. Instead I devote an hour and twenty minutes to composing letters to the Jacksons. By half-past three I am glad it's Georgina's job. But I am still so wound-up that I almost miss my bus stop. I jump off just in time and crash straight into Martin and Jack.

'What are you doing here? What's wrong?'

'Nothing's wrong!' laughs Martin. 'We just thought it would be nice to kick a ball round the park for a while. D'you want to come?'

I can think of a thousand ways to say no, but for some reason my mouth says, 'OK then.' And, I'll be honest, it feels good to run around. Clears my head.

On the way home, Martin asks us if there's anything we'd like to do this weekend, as he's free both days. I say I'll give it some thought, and he looks really pleased!

I get through my homework, supper, and about three telly programmes avoiding all thoughts of starving children, letters to grandparents and tuberculosis. But as I pull off my school clothes, a worse worry hits me: how much Victorian time has passed since last night?

I hang the sign on my door, open my window and climb out. Straddling the two sills I look across and I actually catch the streetlights sort of dissolving! Then Georgina shins up my drainpipe and I nearly slip off the windowsill in shock.

'Have you managed to write to the Jacksons yet?' I ask, as I get my balance back.

'I sent the letter over a week ago, but I've had no reply!'

'What did you write?'

'I did struggle with it, rather,' admits Georgina, easing herself up on to the sill next to me, 'but in the end I simply told them they would have to make haste if they did not want their grandchildren to end up in the grave like their mother. I also told them that James Barker is very dangerous and not to come alone.'

'Yeah! That sounds good,' I say. 'Let's hope they get it!'

We climb into Mary's room, and she is lying in her usual place. 'Hello, Mary,' whispers Georgina brightly. 'I've brought you some broth, and it's still warm! Georgina pulls off a bag she has strapped to her back, and takes out a silver flask and a wooden bowl. She pours this brownish liquid into the bowl, helps Mary sit up a little and lifts it to her lips.

Mary drinks. She looks a bit better. My heart begins to lift. Maybe she will be all right.

While she sips the soup, Georgina tells her bits of news. There are blackbirds nesting in the tree outside her house. There's a new lamplighter their maid Molly is quite keen on. Girl stuff.

I decide now might be a good time to go and check on the other children. 'I have food for them, too,' says Georgina as I leave. 'I'll bring it down shortly!'

I find Jimmy under the stairs as usual. He's crouched in a corner and jumps when I come in. But his face breaks into a smile when he realises it's me. 'Ben—' He doesn't finish what he's saying because the front door suddenly slams and we hear his dad's footsteps thundering up the stairs.

'Mary! I need money, and I need it now! I know you've got some hidden somewhere. You'd better give it to me or you'll be sorry.'

Jimmy and I exchange horrified looks and I leave the cupboard through the hole in the ceiling to try and get up to Mary's room quicker. What's he going to do to Mary, and what will he do when he finds Georgina there?

I get to the bedroom door just behind James Barker. Georgina has one leg out of the window, and he's seen her. 'Who are you and what d'yer think you're doing here?' He grabs her pinafore and she's screaming.

Then there's the sound of shouting below. I run towards the window, and I can see a pair of enormous horses pulling a carriage. Several people are running towards the house; two of them are wearing uniforms.

Barker has seen them too. 'Get off my land!' he shouts down to them, as people start to swarm up his front path. Now they're banging on the door, but he ignores them. All his anger is suddenly fixed on Georgina.

'You brought them here didn't you, girl?' She is trying to wriggle out of his grip and back on to the windowsill, but he holds fast to her dress and hauls her back down.

'Let me go!' she screams, but this makes him more angry. He raises his hand and hits her across the face. She loses her balance and falls against the wall. He goes to hit her again, but Mary somehow springs off her mattress towards him. 'Father, leave her!'

In her hand Mary is holding the wooden soup bowl, which she hurls at his head. It catches him on the ear. He roars, and lets go of Georgina's dress. Georgina scrambles for the window and is nearly out when he is after her again. She jumps across to my windowsill, but he follows her.

'You little witch!' he screams as his heavy feet straddle the two sills. He grabs her dress. He's got her! He starts pulling her back towards him.

Her hands are clinging on to my window frame, but they're slipping...

And then quite suddenly he loses his footing. He lets go of Georgina's dress and grabs for the drainpipe, but not quickly enough. His hand clutches air, and he's falling...

•

Mary and I join Georgina at the window, and we watch in a kind of daze as the crowd on the ground gathers around the dead-still body of James Barker. A man crouches down to listen for breathing, but after a few moments of concentration he shakes his head.

I don't know whether it's seconds or minutes that we stand there, gazing down on this calm and quiet scene as if from a great distance. And it begins to seem impossible that only moments ago James Barker had been at the centre of a much more frenzied, violent one.

Mary reaches for Georgina's hand, and it is as though that small movement suddenly draws the focus of the people gathered below. They look up, and begin talking and pointing.

The two uniformed men burst into action, and start forcing the front door. There's the sound of splintering wood, as the door gives way. Pretty soon the inside of the house is echoing with thundering footsteps and exclamations.

'Look at the state of this!'

'Lord help us, have you seen what's in here?'

'How many children are we looking for?'

'Good God – how is this possible?'

One by one the children are found, and they all support each other in the middle of the dining room, looking fearfully about as the crowd of adults assemble around them. Georgina stands with them, her arms protectively around them, whispering soothingly.

A man with a top hat and a woman in a bonnet step out of the crowd, and move tentatively towards the little huddle of children.

Mary watches them, and then her eyes widen and fill with tears, 'G-Grandmama? Grandpapa?' And she walks unsteadily towards them, her arms outstretched.

The woman lets out a small sob and says, 'Mary?'

They stand for a second, uncertain, and then suddenly they move together and are clinging on to one another. Then the twins run to join them. Only Jimmy stands back, head down. But Georgina pulls him towards his grandfather, and says, 'Mr Jackson, this is Jimmy,' and Mr Jackson takes both Jimmy's hands in his and says gruffly, 'Jimmy, we're taking you home!'

Georgina and I watch as the children are helped into the carriage that is standing outside the house. Just as the horses pull away, Jimmy shouts, 'Goodbye, Georgina and Ben, our two guardian angels!' and Georgina and I burst out laughing because none of the grown-ups can see me, and look completely mystified.

Then it is quiet again. The children have gone, James Barker has gone. It is just Georgina and me, sitting on the wall outside the house gazing down the empty street

'D'you think they'll be all right, Georgina?'

'I think so,' she says in a quiet voice.

'But Mary—' I can't bring myself to tell Georgina what I know, but Georgina looks me straight in the eyes and says, 'I know Mary's very sick, Ben. But she can get better, I'm sure she can... Anyway, she can't die of consumption because I'm going to bore her to death with all the letters I'm going to write!'

I grin, but my grin freezes when she adds, 'But I can't write to you, can I?'

'Hey,' I say flippantly. 'We live opposite each other, we don't need to write letters!'

'True!' she laughs. 'So I'll see you tomorrow then?'

'I'll be waiting!'

'Bye then, Georgina.'

'Goodbye, Ben!'

Slowly I go back into Jimmy's house, up the stairs, through Mary's window, and cross the sills. Outside my bedroom window, I look down to the ground and Georgina is still standing there looking up at me. She doesn't wave, she doesn't turn away, she just stands there becoming gradually less and less solid until at last she has completely faded away. And somehow I know then that I have seen her for the last time.

Chapter Sixteen

It's the end of term (yeah!) and I have read my school report on the bus – it's not bad! Mrs Shah says she thinks I've got a 'good, scientific brain'. Can't wait to show Mum and Martin.

OK, I know: Mum and Martin. All cosy and nice, eh? Well, to be truthful, life with Martin isn't that bad. I mean, he still dresses way uncool, and I wish he'd get a haircut, but he's pretty good at Maths, and helps with my homework, which is quite handy really.

He's not my dad, of course, but then my dad's not much of a dad when you think about it. He still hasn't shown us his BMW, and d'you want to know something? It doesn't seem that important any more.

So, anyway, here I am running from the bus stop up our street, re-reading my school report, when I crash straight into old Mrs Rose. Her stick and my school report go flying. Luckily she doesn't! She totters for a moment but just about manages to stay upright.

'Oops, sorry!' I mumble, gathering our stuff off the pavement.

She suddenly grabs my shoulder and her face

goes white. Oh no! I've given her a heart attack! She is pointing a shaking finger at my report. 'Is your name really Benjamin Ryder?'

Uh-oh! What have I done now? 'Ye-e-s...' I say cautiously.

'Oh my goodness!' she whispers. 'I have something for you.'

And I am following her into her house, completely baffled. She leans on the mantelpiece for a moment, to recover her breath, and then slowly makes her way over to a corner chest. She opens a heavy drawer and pulls out a shabby old cardboard box and tips out the contents. Brownish photos spill out, and suddenly I see a familiar face – 'Georgina!'

She turns to me sharply, her eyes wide. 'So, it's true then,' she says. She takes all the photos from the box and lays them out on the table, and suddenly I am not just looking at photos of Georgina, but of Mary, Jimmy, Annie and Joe! Only they're almost unrecognisable! Because they look healthy and happy! I just stare at the pictures and it's like the best ending of the best film you've ever seen.

But it isn't the end, because Mrs Rose is pulling out an envelope that has been wedged at the bottom of the box. Written on the front of the envelope are two words:

BENJAMIN RYDER

My fingers shake as I open the letter. I know who it's from, of course. I somehow knew she'd think of a way to make contact again. And although I only saw her about four weeks ago, this letter is well over a hundred years old. Aargh! My brain can't handle it! How could hers?

9th September 1890

Dear Ben,

If you are reading this letter, then my guess is correct. I only wish I had the satisfaction of knowing I was right!

There were so many questions I wanted to ask you about your world and time, but I suppose I will have to be satisfied with all the questions I have about my own. I have persuaded father to let me go off to boarding school where I intend to learn all I can about the Physical Sciences, for they will surely unlock the answers to all these mysteries!

Aren't these photographs thrilling? Mary is still a little weak, but the doctors are very encouraging. The twins are so robust you would never know how they had suffered, and Jimmy has taken to life on the farm as to the manner born!

And so, Ben, I must bid you farewell a last time. I do hope your life will be as full of adventure as I believe mine will be.

With love from your friend,
Georgina

I fold the letter carefully. Old Mrs Rose is watching me through her filmy grey eyes, and I know we have loads to talk about.

But not now. Now I need some time. Alone.

•

P.S. Hey! Mrs Rose's grandaughter arrived yesterday. I saw her from my bedroom window. She looks OK. A bit like Georgina actually. Might go over and say, 'Hi'…